Do You Smell Smoke?

A Story About Safety With Fire

Written by
Cindy Leaney

Illustrated by
Peter Wilks

Rourke
Publishing LLC
Vero Beach, Florida 32964

Before you read this story, take a look at the front cover of the book. Do you see smoke?

1. What do you think Emily and Makayla are going to do?

2. How does this show they are practicing fire safety?

Produced by SGA Illustration and Design
Designed by Phil Kay
Series Editor: Frank Sloan

www.rourkepublishing.com

Library of Congress Cataloging-in-Publication Data

Leaney, Cindy.
    Do you smell smoke? : safety with fire / by Cindy Leaney ; illustrated by Peter Wilks.
        p. cm.-- (Hero club safety)
    Summary: Emily and Makayla help prevent disaster when they notice smoke coming from a neighbor's yard.
    ISBN 1-58952-741-0
     [1. Fire extinction--Fiction. 2. Fire prevention--Fiction. 3. Safety--Fiction.] I. Wilks, Peter, ill. II. Title.

PZ7.L46335Do2003
    [E]--dc21

                                                                                    2003043234

Printed in the USA
MP/W

Welcome to The Hero Club!
Read about all the things that happen to them.
Try and guess what they'll do next.

www.theheroclub.com

"What time did José and Matt say they were coming?"

"Anytime now. We still have plenty of time."

"Yeah. Does your neighbor have a fireplace?"

"No. Smoke! Look!"

"Go tell my mom. I'll knock on their door!"

"Right!"

"Hello! Mr. and Mrs. Griffin!
Fire!"

10

11

"Mrs. Harris! There's a big fire
in the backyard next door!"

"Where's Emily?"

"She's knocking on their door. Should I dial 911?"

"Mr. Griffin! Quick—there's a fire in your backyard!"

"Em, help me close all the windows. Kayla, can you take Amy outside? Quick!"

"Come on, Amy. Don't be afraid.
Let's go look at the fire truck."

"What's going on?"

"Is anybody hurt?"

"No, we're okay. Thanks to these two."

23

"Mr. Griffin was burning leaves in his backyard. He went inside and fell asleep, I guess."

"Emily and I smelled smoke."

"These are the girls."

"Girls, do you know what you did today?"

"Did we do something wrong?"

"Not at all. The back of the house was about to catch fire when we got here."

"Thanks, girls. You saved our house.
You may have saved my life."

Was it a good idea for Emily to knock on her neighbor's door?

Why or why not?

IMPORTANT IDEAS

On page 18, Emily's mom says, "Em, help me close all the windows. Kayla, can you take Amy outside? Quick!"

Why did she close the windows? Why did she ask Makayla to take Emily's little sister outside?

Do you know what to do if there is a fire?

Now that you have read this book, see if you can answer these questions:

1. On page 4 you can see something in the picture before you read about it in the story. What is it?

2. What does Makayla tell Emily's mother? And what does Makayla want to do?

3. What happens when the firemen get to the house?

About the author

Cindy Leaney teaches English and writes books for both young readers and adults. She has lived and worked in England, Kenya, Mexico, Saudi Arabia, and the United States.

About the illustrator

Peter Wilks began work in advertising, where he developed a love for illustration. He has drawn pictures for many children's books in Great Britain and in the United States.

HERO CLUB SAFETY SERIES

Do You Smell Smoke? (A Book About Safety with Fire)

Help! I Can't Swim! (A Book About Safety in Water)

Home Sweet Home (A Book About Safety at Home)

Long Walk to School (A Book About Bullying)

Look Out! (A Book About Safety on Bicycles)

Wrong Stop (A Book About Safety from Crime)